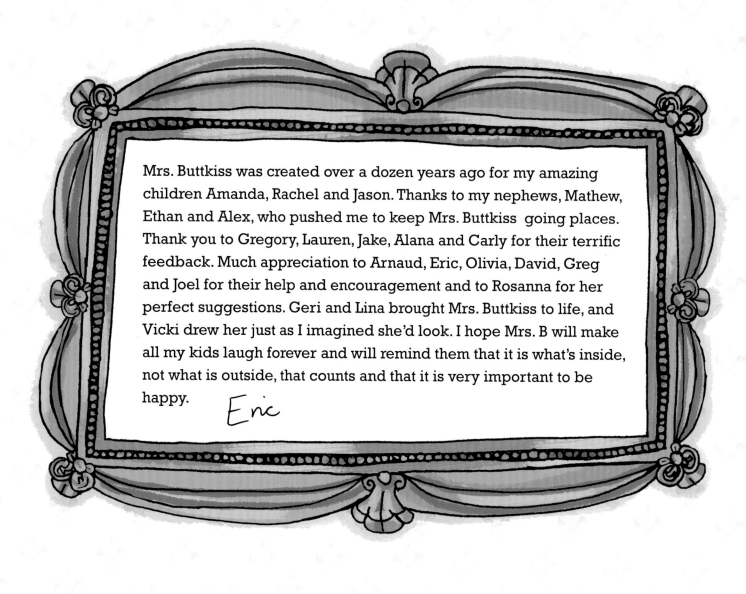

Mrs. Buttkiss was created over a dozen years ago for my amazing children Amanda, Rachel and Jason. Thanks to my nephews, Mathew, Ethan and Alex, who pushed me to keep Mrs. Buttkiss going places. Thank you to Gregory, Lauren, Jake, Alana and Carly for their terrific feedback. Much appreciation to Arnaud, Eric, Olivia, David, Greg and Joel for their help and encouragement and to Rosanna for her perfect suggestions. Geri and Lina brought Mrs. Buttkiss to life, and Vicki drew her just as I imagined she'd look. I hope Mrs. B will make all my kids laugh forever and will remind them that it is what's inside, not what is outside, that counts and that it is very important to be happy.

Eric

I hope you enjoy Mrs. Buttkiss!

Mrs Buttkiss
and the
Big Surprise

by Eric Rosenfeld
Illustrations by Vicki Gausden

Mrs. Buttkiss had a **big** problem.

She had a terrible case of gas. Forever. She was afraid to let it out, because she had no idea what would happen.

Mrs. Buttkiss was a very large woman. She also had a

humongous butt.

So she worried there would be a huge explosion if she farted after holding it in all those years.

Mr. Buttkiss didn't live with Mrs. Buttkiss anymore.

He moved out because he, too, was afraid what would happen when she couldn't hold it in any longer, and he didn't know how to help her.

They didn't have kids, so Mrs. Buttkiss lived **alone**.
Except for her peekapoo Sashimi who loved her, no ifs, ands or buts.

People often stopped and stared when Mrs. Buttkiss walked by because she was so huge. They didn't know about her problem. She kept that to herself.

Until the day they **all** found out.

Mrs. Buttkiss liked to **eat**. She also liked to shop. Every Tuesday, she would walk to the grocery, fill two carts with food, then go home to eat.

On this particular Tuesday, she was filling her second cart and she had just entered the fruit aisle. Suddenly, an irresistible urge came over her.

You can guess what she **wanted** to do.

What she **needed** to do.

As she passed the cantaloupes,
Mrs. Buttkiss finally let go.

Years and years of **fart** escaped with a tremendous blast. The sound was deafening. It was the loudest and longest fart ever recorded in history. The supermarket shook. Food fell onto the floor.

People yelled, unsure what had happened.

Then the smell began to spread. It seemed like a mixture of rotten eggs, dead skunks and old poo. Customers tried to run towards the doors, but no one made it. Everyone in the store fainted before they could escape.

Except Mrs. Buttkiss.

She stood as still as a

statue,

watching the commotion
around her.

She couldn't smell her own fart, but she saw what it did to everyone else. She was scared, so she left her shopping carts, slowly moved around all the people who had passed out and headed towards the exit.

Once back at her apartment, Mrs. Buttkiss felt wonderful. Her stomach felt relieved too. She couldn't believe that she hadn't farted **years** ago.

She couldn't smell her own fart, but she saw what it did to everyone else. She was scared, so she left her shopping carts, slowly moved around all the people who had passed out and headed towards the exit.

Once back at her apartment, Mrs. Buttkiss felt wonderful. Her stomach felt relieved too. She couldn't believe that she hadn't farted **years** ago.

At about the same time, people began to awaken at the grocery store. One by one, they stood up and looked around.

The store smelled

awful.

But **something else** had happened.

Every fruit had changed **color**.

Lemons were red. Oranges were green.
Apples were orange with white polka dots.
Cherries were yellow. Bananas were purple
with yellow stripes. Plums were white.

Customers ran for the beautiful fruit and began piling it in their shopping carts. In just a few minutes, the shelves were bare.

Long lines **quickly** formed at the checkout counters.

The store manager knew what had happened. The big lady's fart had changed the color of the fruit. He had to find her to make more of it.

But **nobody** knew where she was.

Word spread around town about the **fruit**, and the next day, hundreds of people rushed to the store to buy it.

Determined to find Mrs. Buttkiss, the manager posted a sign in the window:

A week later, when she thought no one would remember her or the trouble she caused, Mrs. Buttkiss returned to the grocery to shop. The sign on the door stopped her in her tracks. She knew it was written to her. "They're really mad at me," she thought.

Mrs. Buttkiss went in and timidly asked for the manager. When he appeared, she told him, "My name is Mrs. Buttkiss, and I was the one who farted last week. I am very sorry."

She couldn't believe what happened next.

The manager gave her a big hug. The best he could, because he was a small man and she was a large woman.

A very
large
woman.

"Thank you for coming back," he gushed.
"We're out of colored fruit."

Mrs. Buttkiss was confused, but the manager explained that her fart changed the color of all the fruit. It tasted better than ever and customers were begging for more.

You'll never

guess

what happened next.

The manager offered Mrs. Buttkiss a job farting in the store at night. That way, nobody would faint and she could still color the fruit.

"I can sell your fruit for three times the price of regular fruit, and I can pay you very well," the manager promised.

Mrs. Buttkiss decided
to take the job.

Now she goes to the store every night after dinner and farts in the fruit aisle. When she sees the bananas and grapes, pineapples and oranges, plums and melons, lemons and limes change colors, her work is done.

The customers are happy. The manager is happy.

And Mrs. Buttkiss is very, very happy.

ISBN-13: 978-0-615-31228-6

Library of Congress Control Number: 2009939622

Printed and bound in the United States of America

April 2010 First Edition